MR. MOUSTACHE

originated by Roger Hargreaves

Written and illustrated by Adam Hargreaves

Grosset & Dunlap
An Imprint of Penguin Random House

Mr. Moustache has a moustache, a quite splendid moustache, and Mr. Moustache is a gentleman.

A gentleman is polite and helpful and thoughtful and generous.

And Mr. Moustache was all these things.

And all these things made him wise.

A wisdom he likes to share with his friends.

He taught that a gentleman always tells the truth . . . even about the one that got away!

And Mr. Moustache taught that a gentleman is unrushed and calm . . . even when he is late for kickoff.

On the first of November, Mr. Moustache went to the barber for a trim.

It was so comfortable in the barber's chair that he fell asleep.

But when the barber had finished, Mr. Moustache woke up to a terrible shock.

There in the mirror was a reflection of himself, a reflection that had no moustache.

The barber had shaved him clean!

And as the week went on, Mr. Moustache discovered that this was not the only difference.

For instance, when he left the baker's he let the door slam shut on Mr. Nosey's nose.

When he went to Mr. Perfect's house for tea, he did not bother to wipe his feet.

And when he met Little Miss Splendid, he told her exactly what he thought of her new hat.

"Oh dear," said Mr. Moustache to himself. "What has happened to me? Losing my moustache has stopped me from being a gentleman!"

Fortunately for Mr. Moustache, moustaches grow back.

And as it grew, Mr. Moustache found that he became more and more his old gentlemanly self.

Looking at his slowly growing moustache each day in the mirror, Mr. Moustache had an idea.

Maybe growing a moustache might help some of his other friends.

Some of his other friends who could learn some manners.

So he persuaded his friends to each grow a moustache with him in November.

And as his friends' moustaches grew, so their behavior changed.

Even Mr. Grumpy became a little more of a gentleman!

And by the last day in November, Mr. Moustache was back to his old polite, thoughtful, helpful, and generous self.

And all his friends had the most splendid moustaches.

Particularly, Mr. Silly.

However, the less said about Mr. Sneeze's effort the better!

YUCK!

Now, although Mr. Moustache was back to his old self, there was one new thing in his life.

He had learned a new lesson.

Never fall asleep at the barber's!

————————— MOVEMBER —————————

The month formerly known as November is a moustache-growing charity event held each year to raise funds and awareness for men's health around the world. Real Mr. Men grow real moustaches.

www.movember.com

Mo Bros